For JJ & Ethan - It's fun watching your dreams becoming reality!
- JM

For Dash & Canon. Your Daddy loves ya!
- ML

For information regarding permissions, write to SKOOB BOOKS,
Attention: Permissions Department, PO Box 631183, Littleton, CO 80163

Thrid Printing
2010

SKOOB BOOKS
PO Box 631183
Littleton, CO 80163
www.justinmatott.com

Matott, Justin.
Ludy, Mark.
When I Was A Boy... I Dreamed/Justin Matott; illustrations by Mark Ludy. 3rd Ed.
p. cm.
Summary: An old man tells of the extraordinary dreams he had as a young boy.
But were they dreams at all, or perchance tales from an amazing life still being lived
by an unassuming, little man with a cane...

Library of Congress Control Number: 2004105716
ISBN 1-889191-26-3

Printed by Everbest Printing Co., Nansha, China
Production Date: June 2010
Batch #: 1

WHEN I WAS A BOY I DREAMED

WRITTEN BY

JUSTIN MATOTT

ILLUSTRATED BY

MARK LUDY

SKOOBBOOKS
publishing house
colorado

When I was a boy...

I dreamed

Big Dreams!

I ventured far and near,

and dreamed of great exploring.

Of those dreams you will now hear...

I dreamed I lived up in a tree,

way above the earth below.

Not just in any sort of tree,

in a tree house you should know!

I dreamed I explored the jungles

for the rarest kind of beast,

fought off snakes and gorilla gangs

as I hunted for my feast.

I dreamed I dug to China,

burrowed 'till my back was sore.

And when I hit the other side,

met a Chinese man, then millions more...

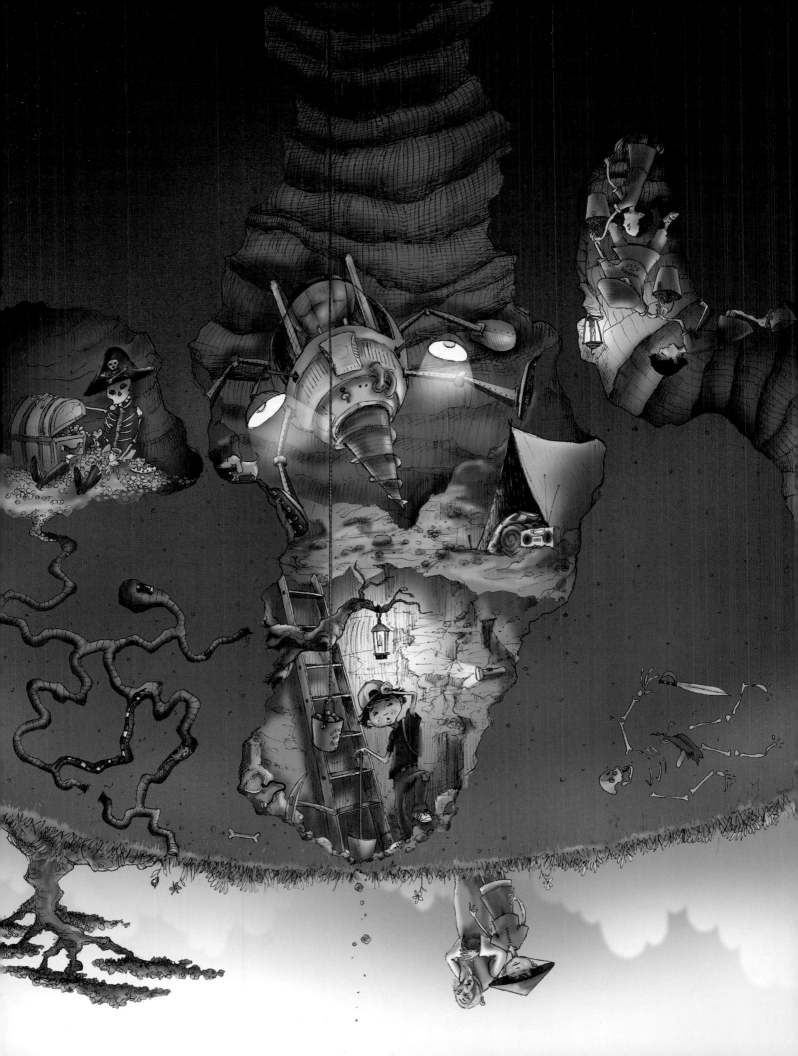

I dreamed I built a rocket ship,

and made a spacey suit.

I blasted up... oh so high...

in my rocket I would shoot.

I banged and pieced together

all sorts of rocket parts.

I brought in steel and cushions;

I wheeled them in by carts.

I dreamed I found the treasure,

the end of the rainbow at last.

A Leprechaun guarded the pot of gold,

I had to think up something fast...

I dreamed I saved a maiden

captured by a dragon mean.

We fought and fought some more

as I battled for that future queen.

I dreamed of ocean battles,

on the high seas I was boss.

We'd hunt down evil pirates,

them off their bow I'd toss.

I chased off all those buccaneers,

the worst was Fearsome Frank.

In his stripey, little underwear,

I made him walk the plank!

I dreamed I ran an ice cream shop,

every flavor you could find.

And if it wasn't there, I'd make

whatever came into your mind!

I dreamed I was a hero,

a firefighter sure and brave!

I'd climb the highest ladder,

those in peril I would save!

I dreamed I built a submarine

to reach the deepest deep,

I'd explore the underwater world

for what may lurk and creep.

I brawled with an eight-legged beast

who fought with all his might.

We wrestled and we battled

for weeks, both day and night.

I dreamed I was a football star,

and touchdowns were my goal.

I played with all my heart and might!

The champion of the Superbowl.

I dreamed I was a one-man-band,

played each instrument you know...

Had crowds and fans at every stop

where I'd put on my show!

I dreamed I roamed the lonesome plains,

way out in the Old West.

In my cowboy jeans and fancy hat,

and my official sheriff vest.

I showed up there right at high noon

and stopped a robber cold.

He tried to hold up the bank,

but now he ain't so bold!

Well, that's all the time we have for now.

I hope you enjoyed your stay.

Come on back sometime soon,

to hear of the whale I rode today.

So many dreams and great adventures,

still for you to hear about!

But I will say, "So long, goodbye,"

yes, for now...